by Sue Graves and Tom Disbury

W
FRANKLIN WATTS
LONDON•SYDNEY

It was the summer holidays.

Anna and Tomek were very excited.

They were going on holiday to France
with Mum and Dad.

Best of all, they were going on a ferry.

They'd never been on a ferry before!

"But what about our car?" asked Tomek,

"can we take take it on a ferry?"

"Yes we can," replied Dad. "A ferry can

take us and our car to France. It is a huge boat."

The port was very busy.

"That's our ferry over there," said Mum.

"It's enormous!" said Tomek, excitedly.

Mum joined a line of cars waiting

to get on board.

"Who are those people?" asked Anna.

"They are some of the crew," said Dad.

"They are going to show Mum

where to park."

Anna, Tomek, Mum and Dad went up on deck. There were lots of passengers.

"Let's get some drinks at the cafe," said Mum.

Just then, Anna spotted a woman in a uniform heading towards them.

"Welcome onboard," said the woman.

"I'm Jenny. I'm one of the crew. We help run the ferry and show you where everything is. If you ever need help, just come and find me."

Dad got everyone some drinks.

Then he and Mum read their books.

Anna and Tomek drew pictures, but they soon got bored.

"Can we go to the gift shop, Mum?" asked Anna.

"It's very busy. You might get lost," said Mum, looking worried.

"I promise I'll keep hold of Tomek's hand all the time," said Anna.

"All right," said Mum, "but be careful."

"Come on Tomek," said Anna, taking his hand.

"Let's go!"

The gift shop was very full of passengers.

It was hard to see through the crowd.

"The toys are over there," said Anna,

pushing her way through.

Tomek spotted a toy ferry.

"I wish I had that," he said.

"I'll buy it for you," said Anna. "Come on."

As Anna lined up to pay, she looked

at her watch.

"We've been a long time, Tomek," she said.

"We'd better go back to Mum and Dad.

They'll be worried about us."

But when they got outside the shop, everything looked different!

"I think the cafe is this way," said Anna, pointing along the deck. Then she stopped and turned around. "Or is it this way?"

"Are we lost?" asked Tomek, looking upset.

"No," said Anna. "Come on, I'm sure the cafe is this way."

They walked and walked but soon Anna
began to worry.

"I'm sure the cafe was nearer than this,"
she said.

"We are lost!" said Tomek and he began to cry.

"Don't cry," said Anna, giving him a hug.

"I'll get you back to Mum and Dad, I promise."

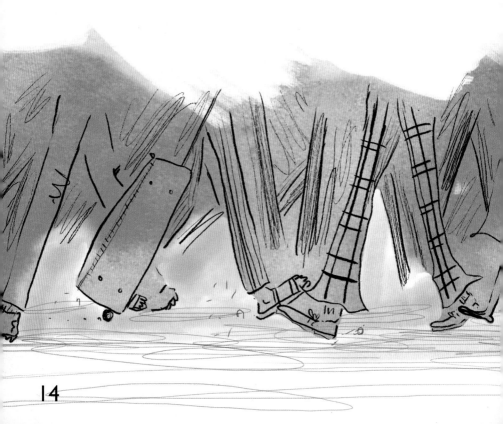

Anna looked around her.

She wanted to ask someone for help.

But who could she ask?

The ferry was full of strangers.

And Mum told her never to talk to strangers!

Just then, Anna saw Jenny.

Jenny looked down at Anna and Tomek, smiling.

"Hello you two," she said.

"Are you ok?"

"We are lost," said Anna. "Mum and Dad are in the cafe. But I can't find the cafe anywhere."

"Don't worry," said Jenny. "I know where it is. Follow me."

Jenny took them to the cafe.

"Oh there you are!" said Dad.

"We were getting worried about you."

"The children were lost," explained Jenny,

"but they told me where to find you."

"Thank you, Jenny," said Mum.

"Don't worry," said Jenny. "It's my job to help people. I keep watch to check no one gets lost."

Just then the ferry's horn sounded.

"We're about to arrive in France," said Jenny.

"I hope you have a lovely holiday."

She smiled at Anna. "And don't get lost again!"

Story order

Look at these 5 pictures and captions.
Put the pictures in the right order
to retell the story.

1

Anna and Tomek become lost.

2

Anna recognises one of the crew.

3

The family is back together.

4

The family pack for their holiday.

5

Mum drives on to the huge ferry.

Independent Reading

This series is designed to provide an opportunity for your child to read on their own. These notes are written for you to help your child choose a book and to read it independently.

In school, your child's teacher will often be using reading books which have been banded to support the process of learning to read. Use the book band colour your child is reading in school to help you make a good choice. *Lost!* is a good choice for children reading at White Band in their classroom to read independently.

The aim of independent reading is to read this book with ease, so that your child enjoys the story and relates it to their own experiences.

About the book

Anna and Tomek have never been on holiday before. They can't wait to get a car ferry to France. Once aboard, they pop to the gift shop, but then have trouble finding their way back to Mum and Dad. Luckily, some crew members can help.

Before reading

Help your child to learn how to make good choices by asking:
"Why did you choose this book? Why do you think you will enjoy it?"
Look at the cover together and ask: "Who are the main characters of the story? What can you spot about the setting of the story?"
Remind your child that they can break longer words into syllables or sound out letters to make a word if they get stuck.
Decide together whether your child will read the story independently or read it aloud to you.

During reading

Remind your child of what they know and what they can do independently. If reading aloud, support your child if they hesitate or ask for help by telling the word. If reading to themselves, remind your child that they can come and ask for your help if stuck.

After reading

Support comprehension by asking your child to tell you about the story. Use the story order puzzle to encourage your child to retell the story in the right sequence, in their own words. The correct sequence can be found on the next page.

Help your child think about the messages in the book that go beyond the story and ask: "What do you think it feels like to get lost? Who would you ask to help you if you got lost?"

Give your child a chance to respond to the story: "What made Anna think of going to Jenny for help? Could she have asked anyone else? What made Jenny stand out from other people in the crowd?"

Extending learning

Help your child reflect on the story, by asking: "What do you think Anna and Tomek learnt when they got lost? Do you think they will pay more attention to their surroundings on another holiday? What could they do differently next time so they don't get lost?"

In the classroom, your child's teacher may be teaching different kinds of sentences. There are many examples in this book that you could look at with your child, including statements, commands, exclamations and questions. Find these together and point out how the end punctuation can help us understand the meaning of the book.

Franklin Watts
First published in Great Britain in 2018
by The Watts Publishing Group

Series Editors: Jackie Hamley and Melanie Palmer
Series Advisors: Dr Sue Bodman and Glen Franklin
Series Designer: Peter Scoulding

A CIP catalogue record for this book is
available from the British Library.

ISBN 978 1 4451 6270 6 (hbk)
ISBN 978 1 4451 6272 0 (pbk)
ISBN 978 1 4451 6271 3 (library ebook)

Printed in China

Franklin Watts
An imprint of
Hachette Children's Group
Part of The Watts Publishing Group
Carmelite House
50 Victoria Embankment
London EC4Y 0DZ

An Hachette UK Company
www.hachette.co.uk

www.franklinwatts.co.uk

Answer to Story order: 4, 5, 1, 2, 3